TIMELESS

A Collection of Mini Sagas
Edited by Gemma Hearn

First published in Great Britain in 2006 by
Young Writers, Remus House, Coltsfoot Drive,
Peterborough, PE2 9JX
Tel (01733) 890066 Fax (01733) 313524
All Rights Reserved

© Copyright Contributors 2006
SB ISBN 1 84602 544 3

Disclaimer
Young Writers has maintained every effort
to publish stories that will not cause offence.
Any stories, events or activities relating to individuals
should be read as fictional pieces and not construed
as real-life character portrayal.

Foreword

Young Writers proudly presents a showcase of the best mini sagas from up-and-coming writers nationwide.

To write a mini saga - a story told in only fifty words - much imagination and skill is required. *Timeless Tales - A Collection of Mini Sagas* achieves and excels these requirements and this exciting anthology will not disappoint the reader.

The thought, effect and hard work put into each mini saga impressed us all and the task of editing proved challenging, due to the quality of entries received, but was, nevertheless, enjoyable. We hope you are as pleased as we are with the final selection and that you continue to enjoy *Timeless Tales - A Collection of Mini Sagas* for many years to come.

Contents of Writers

Charlotte Rhodes (11)	15
Emma Hardie (13)	16
Katy Hatter (10)	17
Rachael Butterworth (14)	18
Laila Hadjimi (12)	19
Georgina Layton (12)	20
Andrew Anderson-Wilson (11)	21
Cassandra Mychajlowycz (13)	22
Melanie Thomas (14)	23
Paula-Marie Burchett (14)	24
Jazmine James (13)	25
Samantha Rutland (13)	26
Charley Dawson (10)	27
Dominic Celimon (10)	28
Lewis Deegan (10)	29
Danny Murray (10)	30
Bethany Walker (9)	31
Daniel Holliday (11)	32
Carys Thomas (14)	33
Monique Tulloch (15)	34
Rebecca Moore (12)	35
Molly Anscombe (12)	36
J K Rigby (12)	37
Ashlee Shannan Matthews (12)	38
Richard Weaving (11)	39
Sydnie Tucker (11)	40
Christopher Hampson (10)	41
Tashin Rahman (12)	42
Carmen Tran (11)	43

Sana Chaudhry (12)	44
Deanne Rendall (15)	45
Jessica Grainger (13)	46
Sapphire Walker	47
Sarah Palmer (16)	48
Dan Crangle (9)	49
Becky Lees (13)	50
Abigail Reed (12)	51
Hannah Greenstreet (12)	52
Daniel Jobson (8)	53
Heather Warren (16)	54
Lara Meade (16)	55
Maria Goodhew (15)	56
Gwen Owen Jones (11)	57
Tanjila Begum (13)	58
Sierra Gaffney (15)	59
Lanya Kawa (12)	60
Shannon Nash (12)	61
Sarah George (18)	62
Amena Iqbal (14)	63
Jessica McDonnell (11)	64
Amy Jones (10)	65
Nafisah Bhatty (11)	66
Stephen Kennedy (10)	67
Sinthu Sridharan (10)	68
William Findlay (10)	69
Katie Reeve (9)	70
Megan Jack (10)	71
Leah McGrotty (13)	72
Bhanuja Sridharan (13)	73
Cara Hetherington (12)	74

Rebecca Roy (15)	75
Charlie Emsley (13)	76

Chestnut Street CE Primary School, Sleaford

Sophie Hare (9)	77
Mikayla Bandy (10)	78
Joshua Williamson (10)	79
Megan Simmons (9)	80
Harriet Blyton (9)	81
Amy Robinson (10)	82
Jack Ede (10)	83
Mitchell Hunt (10)	84
Callum Brickwood	85
Lucy Baumber (10)	86
Amy Newman (9)	87
Zaine Lamont (10)	88
Matthew Waldeck (9)	89
Toni Tustain (9)	90
Jessica Elliott (9)	91

Fort Hill Community School, Winklebury

Melissa Bale (11)	92
Kim Parrott (11)	93
Melody Welsh (11)	94
Libby Yarney (11)	95

Garstang High School, Garstang

Hannah Shepherd (12)	96
James Burch (13)	97
Lucy Dexeter (13)	98
Hannah Slater (13)	99

Jack Crutcher (13)	100
Beth Symons (12)	101
Reuben Gladwin (13)	102
Alex Knowles (13)	103
Lee Armer (12)	104
Jenny Rawsthorne (12)	105
Alexander Hay (12)	106
Natasha Davies (12)	107
Amy Lewtas (12)	108
Daniel Knox (12)	109
Harry Crooke (12)	110

Glenfield Primary School, Glenfield

Samuel Anderson (9)	111
Charlie Lomas (8)	112
Tuesday Coleman (8)	113
Joshua Scott (8)	114
Tavia Alonzo (8)	115
Matthew Stevens (9)	116
James Etheridge (9)	117
Bethany Marshall (9)	118
Harry Sharman (9)	119

Grundisgburgh Primary School, Grundisburgh

Dale Mortimer (11)	120
Callum Lomas (11)	121
Becky Holifield (10)	122
Emily Witherden (10)	123
Jade Cable (11)	124
George Clark (11)	125
Ben Buffone (11)	126

Heathcote School, Chingford
Jamie Strange (11) 127
Kelly Frank (11) 128
Josh Kimpton (11) 129
Tonmie Lee (11) 130
Bonnie Jack (12) 131
Onoufrios Theodoulou (11) 132
Lewis Bannerman 133
Steven Holmes (11) 134

International School of Düsseldorf, Germany
Niklas Rehmert (13) 135
Nik Baron (13) 136
Malin Bergström (13) 137
Verena Bethke (13) 138
Max Andersen (14) 139
Carolina Sandbrook (14) 140
Martin Shih (13) 141
James Bolton (14) 142
Lisa Jansen (13) 143
Phil Kelly (14) 144
Clare Leake (13) 145
Katerina Trefilov (14) 146
Rory Higgins (14) 147
Niko Blomeyer (13) 148

International School of Paphos, Cyprus
Fiona Schuetze (14) 149
Claire Trippit (13) 150
Eliot Gannon (12) 151
Katherine Courtney (14) 152

Loreto Convent, Kenya
Natalie Kimani (15) 153
Lydia Gachuhi (16) 154
Sarah Itambo (17) 155

Nonsuch High School for Girls, Cheam
Cathryn Antoniadis (12) 156
Amy Tiri (13) 157

Our Lady & St Oswald's Catholic Primary School, Oswestry
Hollie Jones (11) 158
Bethany Griffiths (10) 159
Shannon Graham (10) 160
Sebastian Pierpoint (10) 161

Sacred Heart School, Barrow-in-Furness
Bradley Wright (10) 162
David Davies (10) 163

The Bishop Bell CE Mathematics & Computing Specialist School, Eastbourne
Alice Smith (15) 164
Laura Upton (15) 165
Craig Miller (14) 166
Nikita Butcher (14) 167
Tyler North (13) 168
Joseph Belchem (15) 169
Daniel Bridge (15) 170
Luke Sivers (15) 171

The International School, Ibadan, Nigeria
Sefeoluwa Oyelude (15) 172
Akande Rukayat (15) 173

The Ladies' College, Guernsey
Anna de Carteret (13) 174
Laura Campbell (13) 175
Charlotte Bailey (13) 176
Jocelyn Camm (12) 177
Kelley Cameron (12) 178
Rebecca Ashworth (12) 179
Amelia Brown (12) 180
Aimee Gaudion (12) 181
Emma Hardy (13) 182
Lara Baudains (12) 183
Katherine Dorrity (12) 184
Katie Enevoldsen (12) 185
Chloe Davison (13) 186
Melanie Ayres (12) 187
Sarah Le Mesurier (12) 188
Niamh Hanna (12) 189
Charlotte Giles (13) 190
Amy Baird (11) 191
Rebecca Case (11) 192
Laura Bampton (10) 193
Fenella Gladstone (11) 194
Kirsten Anderson (12) 195
Sophie Caseby (11) 196

Threemilestone School, Truro
Josh Richards (10) 197
Jordan Hansen (10) 198
Craig Jackson (10) 199
James Benney (11) 200
Bethany Howell (10) 201
Lisa Caddy (10) 202
William Bowden (10) 203
Sabina Moss (11) 204
Jack Dyer (10) 205
Jessica Hyland (10) 206

Waldegrave School for Girls, Twickenham
Nikita Vasistha 207
Georgia Hirst (13) 208

The Mini Sagas

MADAME TUSSAUDS

Congratulations Charlotte - your Mini Saga wins you a fantastic family ticket to Madame Tussauds. Here you'll get the chance to get up close to your favourite celebrities at this amazing day out in London. Stars such as Brad Pitt, Wayne Rooney, Robbie Williams, Jennifer Lopez and many more are all under one roof at the tourist attraction everyone is talking about. Have a seat in the Big Brother diary room and chat to Big Brother and Davina, or step on to The Black Pearl and discover The Dead Man's Chest with Captain Jack Sparrow, Will Turner and Elizabeth Swann. Check out their website www.madame-tussauds.co.uk for further information, and we hope you have a terrific visit. Keep on writing!

The Difference

We met as strangers and soon became friends. I, a minstrel, he, explorer. As we walked, two paths diverged. We went our separate ways. A roar, a scream. My friend was dead. For I had taken the road most travelled, and that made all the difference.

Charlotte Rhodes (11)

My Best Friend, The Drunk Driver And Me

She soared through the air, landing in a motionless heap. Just minutes ago she had said, 'You worry too much!' before the car swerved towards her like dodgems at the fairground.
I stroked her milky white hand. 'Don't die,' I sobbed.
Her eyes flickered. 'You worry too much,' she whispered.

Emma Hardie (13)
The Ladies' College, Guernsey

RUNNER UP

Well done Emma! You win a superb reading and writing goodie bag which includes a selection of books and a Staedtler Writing Set.

STAEDTLER

The Darkness Of The Night

Running, he chases me, my heart pounding, through the empty streets. He's a giant swamping the world behind me. I fall. He takes his chance, grabbing me in the blackness.
Suddenly she rescues me, the bright moon frightening the night away, watching me. Her flickering torches guide my pathway home.

Katy Hatter (10)

RUNNER UP

Well done Katy. Your Mini Saga also wins you a reading and writing goodie bag containing a selection of books and a Staedtler Writing Set!

TIMELESS TALES

Legs

He'd tried this jump every day since he'd grown legs, without success.
1 ... 2 ... 3! He jumped the pond, wind rushed past his head. Below all was blue. He landed by a hedge. The small frog hopped towards it with thoughts of snuggling down for his first winter's hibernation, zzz.

Rachael Butterworth (14)

First Time

You lie back. Your muscles tighten. They approach you. They ask if you're afraid but you ignore them. You shiver and your body tenses! After seconds you feel something burn within. You lie panting, glad it's all over. You thank them, after all it's your first time having an injection.

Laila Hadjimi (12)

Aliens!

Going closer, worrying about what to do. I shouldn't be here! I'm forbidden! The world doesn't matter; all my attention is focused on the strange object. I reach out my hand to touch it and a door slides open. A mutant creature crawls out and croaks, 'I won't harm you!'

Georgina Layton (12)

Time To Die!

It came from out of the dark, teeth and claws dripping with blood, its hulking body leaning over them. They are the two samurai of light; it is the creature of death. They look up at the creature, its eyes glaring at them.
'Time to die!'
And the fight begins …

Andrew Anderson-Wilson (11)

Life Is Hard ... Live It To The Fullest

In a café; sad. Jessie comes up; sees I'm sad. She sits. 'Sometimes life is hard and not fun. Other times it's simple and easy to enjoy. If you're happy it will seem like you live longer because you're enjoying life.'

I'm now happy. We leave the café together.

Cassandra Mychajlowycz (13)

Why?

In my room, I remember. Reading my magazine, following fashions, I became obsessive. I made an effort but I just got remarks. I'm ugly, fat, a geek. Plastic surgery, diet, I threw away my life. I had nothing left. Hell awaited me. Gun to my head, I pulled the trigger.

Melanie Thomas (14)

Jane, Sophie And Lucy Go Through The Plughole

With a splash, they were there. Glittering water surrounded them, mermaids everywhere. They heard a blood-curdling yell. Suddenly, out of nowhere, the black atrocity appeared, grabbing and pulling at them. They had to escape. They struggled and fought. At the last moment they were pulled to safety.

Paula-Marie Burchett (14)

The Killer's Last Kill

'Did you hear that?'
'No! Come on, we'll be late.'

The door screeches.

'Mattie! I know I heard that!'

'Well I didn't! Let's go!'

Bang!
They both jump and look at each other.

'Look out!'
'Oh no! Someone help!'

Mattie's bleeding on the floor …
And so's the killer!

Jazmine James (13)

Good Memories Are The Things That Make Memories

It was painfully quiet in the departure lounge. But somehow it was the most chaotic atmosphere. 'Anyone sat here?' a familiar voice asked, but I just couldn't place it.

That was the day which created a memory, which will always be fresh in my mind and never fading.

Samantha Rutland (13)

The Explosion

Alone ... Professor Hicks furiously searched for an answer, he mixed the poisonous liquids. Gas spread gently, the professor felt nervous. As the experiment bubbled the professor panicked, knowing the test was out of his control. Shouting, 'Help!' he sprinted for the door, but just as he got there - *kaboom!*

Charley Dawson (10)

The Friendly Vampire

I was all alone in the park. I felt a breath on my neck. I turned around, nothing was there! I got up, I saw a shadow. I went up to it and found it was my friend. There was something not right about him.
'Ouch!'
Something bit my neck.

Dominic Celimon (10)

The Thief

Driving in my car. Stop for fuel, leave my car open, no one's there. Pay, have a quick chat with John - he said that was his name. He tells me, 'Never leave your car open while you're gone!'
Go to car it's gone!

Lewis Deegan (10)

Viking Invasion

In the Viking invasion of Britain there was a big, big, big battle in Wessex. There was the sound of blood being spilled and swords clashing against each other. But eventually the British *won* and Britain was free.

Danny Murray (10)

The Mystery

It was a dark night. Sitting down on the bed after dark, the girl next door moaned horribly. It was strange - she did it every night!

I lay down. A flash and a puff of smoke filled the air. The girl cackled, all was dark and I was petrified!

Bethany Walker (9)

Scuba Diving

The sea was glimmering in the sunlight. I dived into the sea, it rippled, then I swam down to the bottom, the fish swarmed around me. Their colours amazed me.
Then all of a sudden there was blood. I heard a snap of jaws and I saw a body.

Daniel Holliday (11)

Devastation!

I ran increasing in speed, faster and faster, knowing I was being followed. They were gaining on me. I tried to escape, dodging left, stepping right. Then I saw it. Did my eyes deceive me? Still for the line I strived. Suddenly I hit the ground, I'd been tackled!

Carys Thomas (14)

Untitled

Running across the terrain, heat beating upon my brow. I stumble over rocks, grazing my hands and feet as I crash to the ground. My hands ball into fists. Gentle hands grip my arms and lift me. I cannot repress the smile as I see her face.
'You're safe now.'

Monique Tulloch (15)

Death On The Cliff

The fair maiden called to her love, 'Don't leave me darling!'
'I'm sorry,' he cries, and jumps off the cliff edge.
I watch it all, my heart thumping in my chest. The fair maiden collapses on the floor, sobbing.
'Bravo, bravo,' cries the audience.
'A clear winner,' calls the judge.

Rebecca Moore (12)

Am I Alone?

There I am, right in the middle, people surrounding me. Then suddenly *bam!* I'm on the floor, my eyes blurry. I stagger up onto my feet to see nothing but darkness. I feel a tingle on my back. Now it's on my ankle. I feel a hand. Then suddenly - *gone!*

Molly Anscombe (12)

Just Around The Corner

It was down the back alley that Anna saw them. It was dark and cold, but Anna knew they would see her if she moved. Anna heard a kid's head bang on the brick wall. They punched the kid hard, but stopped suddenly.
'Look guys,' one cackled, 'we've got company …'

J K Rigby (12)

Snow

As I woke up I saw the white, cotton candy snow floating down. When I got changed into my snow clothes, my friends were already out starting a snowball fight. After an hour playing and making snowmen, I got cold so I went in and had a nice hot chocolate.

Ashlee Shannan Matthews (12)

Untitled

They ran like the wind to get away from the sharp fangs, not daring to stop nor look behind. Suddenly one stumbled, and the very thing they had been looking for all their lives, was their own bitter end - a sabre-tooth tiger!

Richard Weaving (11)

Can They Get Out

They searched all around, trying to get out. Night and day they worked together. Strange creepy noises, owls, wolves, trees rustling. They tried to make a fire but the wind was too strong. It was cold, no food. Would they survive? They kept searching. 'Look!' they said. They found daylight.

Sydnie Tucker (11)

It Was Coming!

I heard its footsteps coming closer and closer. Was it going to catch up with me? I had to get away but how? I darted down a nearby alley and hid behind a wheelie bin. A moment later the footsteps stopped. Then … 'Get back 'ere you stupid dog!'

Christopher Hampson (10)

The Venom Death!

I tried to run as fast as possible. I knew I shouldn't have gone out hunting. The cobra reared up hissing. Then I tripped over. The vicious cobra stung his venom into my skin. I closed my eyes, but before I did, I saw a shadow cowering over me.

Tashin Rahman (12)

Mysterious Bang!

The children played all day long, but the next day was different, they heard a bang in the cupboard, then it was on the windows. A couple of children went up to the windows.
Suddenly there was groaning.
The teacher said, 'Stop it children now!'
But it wasn't them.

Carmen Tran (11)

Pirates

Wind howled, water surged over the deck, masts creaked, bullets poured from the sky. Then, our only chance came by the golden hope for survival. Until ... Roger came into view, not seeming too jolly. A thick mist enveloped us. Time seemed to stop. A single cannon blast. Then it happened ...

Sana Chaudhry (12)

The Struggle

The beast growled. I struck it hard upon its muzzle. It lashed out at me. The beast would not be stilled. My futile attempts made it rage. I calmed, became still. The creature grumbled a moment, then it was silent. The sea was tamed by my breeze.

Deanne Rendall (15)

Water

The icy water cascaded my body, the cool droplets engulfed me, drenching me. A jet of frozen air swirled around me. A great powerful waterfall. I reached into the distance. My hand made contact. I turned the pressure down, brushed the curtain aside and stepped out of the shower.

Jessica Grainger (13)

The Champion

The boy was left alone. He was surrounded by bodies, lying there motionless, as if they were asleep. Silence filled the gym. The scent of fear strangled the air. Tears ran down the boy's face. He was the only one left; the boy had won the game of dodgeball.

Sapphire Walker

The Visitor

I couldn't understand what had happened, one minute he was here hovering over me, his stench filling my nostrils until I couldn't breathe, the next he was gone, a blur in the distant sunset. But they wouldn't believe me! No one ever believes it when an alien visits Earth.

Sarah Palmer (16)

Untitled

We felt heat on our backs. Suddenly we flew backwards, we could hear the sound of screaming behind us. I could hear my heart beating like mad! The next moment we got turned upside down. When would it ever stop? A voice said, 'Get off the ride boys!'

Dan Crangle (9)

Nearly There

I was going to be late. I turned the corner. I had to get there in time. I changed gear and quickened the pace. One more corner. Headlights blinding. I didn't see the lorry. One broken leg and whiplash but my daughter won the spelling competition. I wasn't even there.

Becky Lees (13)

Brand New World - Heaven

The crescent moon was shadowed by the head of a stranger, by a sense of mystery. I didn't know who the person was but it wasn't a person, it was an angel. I knew my time had come, time to leave the world behind and enter another.

Abigail Reed (12)

Waiting

Here I am, sitting in a hard-backed chair. Waiting, alone, oh so alone, for what is to come. I tense my muscles, ready for action. It can't be long now. A sudden coldness pervades the room. What I had been waiting for had arrived.

Hannah Greenstreet (12)

A Horrible Time

It looked deep and cold. I heard a *drip … drip …* I grabbed the door and pulled it open *creeeaak*. It was dark. I heard a *drip … drip …* again. What a mess I was in! I want to stay like this anyway! 'Do I have to go in the bath Mum?'

Daniel Jobson (8)

Are You Courting Death?

I met him by the river. He didn't see me there. I followed him home, along the cobbled path, under the cover of night. He turned back and looked me in the eye. 'Hello,' he called.
'Goodbye,' I whispered.
I kissed him softly on the lips. The kiss of Death.

Heather Warren (16)

Battle

And there he stood, amidst the churning bodies,
Watching as the pitted blade hurtled towards him,
the knight's eyes ablaze with the kill. And slowly it
approached, dull and red and sharp. Only a pause
of time left for terror, as slowly, coldly, it came to
rest within his neck.

Lara Meade (16)

Grand Theft Auto

I touched her body, so smooth yet cold. She stood like a horse waiting to be ridden. She belonged to someone else … but rules were made to be broken. I started the engine. Cars are made to be stolen. This baby's here to be driven.

Maria Goodhew (15)

Misty Shroud

Mist, deep and unfathomable, twined lazily across the glass-like lagoon, resembling ethereal limbs. The condensation clung to the rocks and hillocks. Suddenly ... it came. Watching closely, a human *might* discern something pushing through the frosty smog ... But as swiftly as it emerged, the Loch Ness monster disappeared into its domain.

Gwen Owen Jones (11)

Kidnapped!

'Run as fast as you can, don't stop, you have to get away,' screamed the conscious of Aaliyah as she fell down the side of a hill in the woods. She had been kidnapped. Her kidnapper wanted to kill her! Would she ever make it alive or would she die?

Tanjila Begum (13)

Dreams Can Traumatise

A swirling vortex of colour encircles me, making my head swim. The spectacular light show of rainbows fills my eyes, causing them to water. Tears of joy trickle down my cheeks, sparkling like diamonds, twinkling like stars in the sky. I've never been so happy.

I wake up and weep.

Sierra Gaffney (15)

The End Of My Dream

I heard the prison door crash closed, suffocating me in the darkness. This is it, I am damned. Forced to live life against my own will. My destiny shattered in a second of madness. I stared up at the man before me and whispered the words I dreaded, 'I do.'

Lanya Kawa (12)

The Strange Woman

The Vikings set off, heading to the great land. On their travels they came across a woman who said the land they seek is cursed. The Vikings had no time, and left.

Later they arrived, but it was plague-ridden and laden with carcasses. But who was the strange woman?

Shannon Nash (12)

She's A Winner

'Go!' shouts the commentator. She speeds off. Screams come from the crowd as she goes left, right, another right, at over 140km/h. The wind's blowing, snow's falling. She jumps … a huge gasp is heard. Then a roar as she crosses the finish line, landing the final jump to win gold!

Sarah George (18)

The Mystery

Everyone was happy. The crowds were cheering, smiling, laughing and clapping. The presenter was smirking, the cameramen looked happy as ever, but suddenly there was silence. The crowds were absolutely silent. The presenter was speechless as the cameramen looked in absolute disbelief. What was happening? What was it?

Amena Iqbal (14)

Queen Kate

The horses galloped as fast as they could, none of them could catch Queen Kate. She was too fast, the armies just couldn't catch her. The soldiers around her were racing for their lives. Then she saw it, Henry the soldier had died, he was her favourite. She wept.

Jessica McDonnell (11)

Rise To Beauty

Gordon caterpillar scurried down the ruby-red rose stem. He munched contentedly upon a juicy leaf. He lost his grip and fell, landing on a patch of grass. He fumbled around thinking he was lost. Not for long. He flew into the sky as a very pretty lemon-yellow butterfly.

Amy Jones (10)

Untitled

I panicked. I couldn't find a way out. I kept thinking about the ghost in my meaningful dreams. I tried going through every visible door but every door I went through seemed to lead to more misery. I screamed with happiness. I saw it … I saw the magnificent exit door.

Nafisah Bhatty (11)

The Alien

The dark black alien with its sharp antennae sits in the corner. Its one eye flashes with its many strange colours. It scares me, silent except when its brain is awake and ready to explode. Its hypnotising eye paralyses me. I will do whatever it says. 'Watch me, the TV!'

Stephen Kennedy (10)

The Friendly But Vicious-Looking Dog

Darren searched through the night for his best friend Harry. He gasped when he saw a vicious brown dog, dribbling down its scruffy chin. The dog was violently chewing on a piece of meat. With its long sharp canines, when suddenly, it stopped and pounced on Darren. 'Harry, it's you!'

Sinthu Sridharan (10)

The Fight Of Vedluf And The Humans

One day in the land of Death, Vedluf was feeding his twin-headed wolf, Killer. When he told Killer that he had declared war on the humans, Killer started howling with joy. When the day came they went to fight and lost. The humans won because they were better fighters.

William Findlay (10)

The Creature

The eight-legged creature with a black inky blob
in the middle was coming to bite me, to create
a sticky web, have babies with its mate and then
make an army to take over the world.
I grabbed a fly swat and whacked the spider
crawling up my leg.

Katie Reeve (9)

Killing Time

She was just sitting reading, until - *knock, knock*.
'Hello,' she called.
'Gimme the money!'
'Argh, oww!'
The man grabbed the purse. He went away.
'Hello is that the police?'
The man came back and - *bang* ... !

Megan Jack (10)

Middle Of The Night

He started. He heard voices, mumbling and groaning. There was whispering and the sounds of movement. It was the middle of the night, the moon was shining. He shook his head and made a mug of hot chocolate. He finished it and went back to sleep, cuddling into his duvet.

Leah McGrotty (13)

Little Accident

Sarah arrived at school when her mobile rang. Her mother's voice came in a surprise. 'Your little sister's had an accident!'
Skidding past the people, Sarah ran breathlessly until she reached her sister's room. There stood her mother, her face in disgust as she was cleaning the wet, damp bed.

Bhanuja Sridharan (13)

Beware Of The Mermaids

Beware of the mermaids on a full moon night. They will entrance you and take you to a watery grave. To one this meant nothing, but take heed, on a full moon night you hear no scream, just the singing of a mermaid, the splash of a body. Beware. Beware.

Cara Hetherington (12)

Blonde Pigtails, Red Cheeks
And A Wobbly Bottom Lip

Mummy's hand disappeared. Sudden forest of strangers, a dark bewildering unknown. The trembling lip curls into a scream; thunder for the ants below on the granite desert.
'Darling!'
Found by an irritated voice and rescuing hand. Child's helpless fingers wrap around familiar skin and a wedding band.

Rebecca Roy (15)

Homework

Art homework: painting still life. Dog, snoozing on rug. The heavy beat of music comes from my sister's room. Phone rings. 'I'll get it!' It was my friend Amy. Chatted … Put the phone back. Went to continue homework. The dog stared at me, a shred of homework in his mouth.

Charlie Emsley (13)

A Lovely Surprise

It was a cold winter's night and Tommy was fast asleep and dreaming of his beautiful cat Binka who was due to have kittens.
When morning came and Tommy went downstairs, he saw Binka laid proudly with nine kittens sleeping peacefully around her. What a lovely surprise.

Sophie Hare (9)
Chestnut Street CE Primary School, Sleaford

The Little Girl Who Got Lost In The Woods

She walked as slowly as she could trying to get out of the woods. She heard footsteps behind her, which sent a shiver down her spine. She started to run as fast as she could. Then there it was, the end of the woods and her mum was waiting there.

Mikayla Bandy (10)
Chestnut Street CE Primary School, Sleaford

The Vampula Chase

Jim and Bob climbed the extremely rocky mountain as fast as they could to escape from the dreaded Vampula, like a vampire but much worse.
'Where's he gone?' Jim asked Bob.
Bob replied, 'He's fallen off, so let's stop to rest.'
'Finally,' Jim puffed slowly.
That's exactly what they did.

Joshua Williamson (10)
Chestnut Street CE Primary School, Sleaford

Rock Girl Band

The Rock Girls were a band of four. They were competing against The Devils as all the other bands had been eliminated. They were so nervous, but then the announcement came - Bonnie, lead singer of The Devils had lost her voice. The Rock Girls were declared winners of the competition.

Megan Simmons (9)
Chestnut Street CE Primary School, Sleaford

The Bright Light

The bright light grew bigger and bigger. It looked as though it would fall. It gleamed like a star, a beautiful star, it got nearer and nearer, so near it could have surely blinded someone.
Then suddenly it fell, sparks flew off it, then silently landed. It was a unicorn.

Harriet Blyton (9)
Chestnut Street CE Primary School, Sleaford

Cat And Mouse

Fluffy the cat was in a gigantic field. He saw something strange in the distance.
What is it? he thought.
As he walked further, he saw something small and grey. It was a mouse! Fluffy licked his lips and got ready to pounce, however, the mouse escaped - just in time!

Amy Robinson (10)
Chestnut Street CE Primary School, Sleaford

The Match

Three minutes left, the scoreboard read 1-1, the Ruskington Lions really needed to pull together if they wanted to win this match. After a good pep talk from the coach, the players lined up ready for attack, feeling geared up and raring to go!
Game over 2-1 Ruskington Lions.

Jack Ede (10)
Chestnut Street CE Primary School, Sleaford

A Minute Of Magic

Pushing, sliding, diving, sweat, pain. They'd hoped to win the final. He runs, crosses, flicks on. It's a corner. Last minute of the game. He passes, he crosses. The goalie panics. It's a rumble to get it in.
Goal! Birmingham has won the FA Cup. Goal of the season.

Mitchell Hunt (10)
Chestnut Street CE Primary School, Sleaford

Space

This boy called Callum Brickwood had no ideas for his science homework. An hour later he still couldn't come up with any ideas so he went in his pretend space rocket.
Suddenly the pretend rocket took off and flew into space. It was pitch-black and he couldn't see a thing.

Callum Brickwood
Chestnut Street CE Primary School, Sleaford

The Unicorn

The unicorn was trapped, knowing that he would be rescued. He kept on his neighing all day and night, always thinking when would that person come. Until one night, he saw somebody. Who was it? It was his owner, yes it was his owner, he had come to the rescue.

Lucy Baumber (10)
Chestnut Street CE Primary School, Sleaford

Chloe And The Raging Bull

They decided that the quickest way to get to Chloe's house was to cross the field that had the bull in it. It was very scary to climb over the gate and cross to the other side, watching all the time for the bull.
They made it, safe at last.

Amy Newman (9)
Chestnut Street CE Primary School, Sleaford

A Lucky Escape

All four of us were trying to tread water softly as the sharks were trying to attack us, but just in time an octopus distracted the sharks. We swam quickly to a rock island and there above us we all heard the whirling sound of a helicopter. 'Hooray!'

Zaine Lamont (10)
Chestnut Street CE Primary School, Sleaford

The Long Bike Ride

It should have been an easy mountain bike ride but it was up, up and up for five miles and when I thought we had reached the top, it was up, up again. I nearly cried. We finally got the top, then, downhill all the way home.

Matthew Waldeck (9)
Chestnut Street CE Primary School, Sleaford

The Mysterious Man

One day I went for a walk with my friend. We turned a corner, a strange man stood there, he started chasing us. We looked behind, there was no longer a man but just a head floating. We ran as fast as possible not knowing what was there.

Toni Tustain (9)
Chestnut Street CE Primary School, Sleaford

Taking Katie For A Walk

On a cold and frosty morning running across the fields leaving footprints in the snow I saw snow moving in the distance. Running for the tree the snow ran towards me.
Next time I will put Katie's red coat on and not her white fluffy one.

Jessica Elliott (9)
Chestnut Street CE Primary School, Sleaford

The Quest To Chocolate Land

Sam and Sadie were at home when their mum shouted, 'I need you to go to Chocolate Land.' On the journey they met their friends and travelled through sun, rain, wind and snow. Conquering battles they fought the toughest chocolate warrior, before travelling back home to find a great celebration.

Melissa Bale (11)
Fort Hill Community School, Winklebury

Stripe's Missing

After being chased by rhinos Tigger set off to find his mummy. Travelling far, climbing high. Suddenly he faced hyenas, he ran. He saw water with rhinos sleeping so he crept past, drank and sat down under a tree. Hearing a noise Tigger looked up and saw his mummy.

Kim Parrott (11)
Fort Hill Community School, Winklebury

The Quest For The Golden Doughnut

Lady Diamond jumped onto her dragon and flew across the valley for the golden doughnut. Battling out, through mud baths, marshes, parks and swamps. Then suddenly a troll jumped out so she killed him and then took the golden doughnut and she flew back on her dragon safely.

Melody Welsh (11)
Fort Hill Community School, Winklebury

The Quest For The Dior Watch

Mari and her friend Stella wanted a limited edition Dior watch. They went to town and they had to trek through shopping queues and mountains of bags. At the Dior checkout Stella and Mari had to answer a question, 'What is fashion?' Fortunately they knew and got the watch.

Libby Yarney (11)
Fort Hill Community School, Winklebury

Untitled

As I carry the heavy stone on my back to take to my nest, I feel the ground begin to shake. I look up at the huge giants and begin to run, but I am not fast enough, they catch up with me, I know I am going to die.

Hannah Shepherd (12)
Garstang High School, Garstang

Spring

I stand alone, the last of a great army, as my soul disperses amongst the bodies of my fallen comrades, their bodies already rotting on the brown battlefield, our yellow bodies ragged and ramped. But I know next spring we rise again to whistle in the sun and wind.

James Burch (13)
Garstang High School, Garstang

Penalty Shoot-Out

I stood there, my heart pounding, the crowd shouting and screaming my name. I took a long deep breath preparing myself for what was about to happen. Then I started to run, my studs sinking in the ground. *Whack!* It was all over, I had brought disappointment to my team!

Lucy Dexeter (13)
Garstang High School, Garstang

The Ice Cube

It's cold in my home. My friends have all died. The door opens without knowing and I am picked up and taken from my lovely, freezing home. I see liquid swirling in front of me like a black hole. I am dropped in the warm liquid and I slowly die.

Hannah Slater (13)
Garstang High School, Garstang

Spaceman During Landing

I began my descent; there was a shudder, the usual darkness broken. The entry was long and tantalising, my hands and face shaking as the ground became even closer. The sky shrinking, the once small dots on the ground now so ever bigger. The staring faces watching eagerly, how exciting.

Jack Crutcher (13)
Garstang High School, Garstang

The Ocean

I was deep down in the ocean. Tropical fish were swimming around me - all different colours and sizes, hiding from predators and searching for prey. Light was beating down, making everything look even more beautiful. I started to swim up but disaster stuck. I was running out of air. Fast!

Beth Symons (12)
Garstang High School, Garstang

Loneliness

She felt lonely all on her own. She knew eventually she would be found. She was tempted to give herself in but she knew if she did she would still be alone. Searching not hiding though. She heard footsteps. Suddenly the cupboard door burst open. She was no longer alone.

Reuben Gladwin (13)
Garstang High School, Garstang

The Snowman

As I stand frozen with cold, the early morning sun starts to beam onto my back. I feel cold trickles of icy water run from beneath my threadbare scarf. By evening time nothing will be left of me except a hat, a carrot, several pieces of coal and a scarf.

Alex Knowles (13)
Garstang High School, Garstang

Don't Take Me Away

I was petrified, sat there in the corner, waiting for the door to crash open. The door crashed open, jarring it off its hinges. The light streamed into the room. Suddenly, I clinched my eyes shut in fear of being taken away. I shouted for my mum but nobody replied.

Lee Armer (12)
Garstang High School, Garstang

The Graveyard

He walked through the graveyard. The dusty moon shone above, casting eerie shadows on gravestones. A creak rang out through the night. He stopped and looked edgily around him. But it was the moan that really scared him.

The following night, an image of the boy floated around the graveyard.

Jenny Rawsthorne (12)
Garstang High School, Garstang

Goal

I run with it wanting to score, pumping with adrenaline as I reach the goal. I watch and examine his every movement. He begins to hunt me down preparing for my shot. I take it past him and shoot, it rolls into his net. He is beaten.

Alexander Hay (12)
Garstang High School, Garstang

Haunted Down

The white figure floated towards me. What could I do? I went to punch it but my hand went right through. A shiver went up my spine. I backed away, trying to escape. I reached the wall, the door was near me. I grabbed at the handle and ran away.

Natasha Davies (12)
Garstang High School, Garstang

The End

He stood still, frozen to the spot, his heart beating so hard he thought it would come right out of his chest. The skeletal figure was moving closer and closer towards him. The boy opened his mouth to scream but no sound came out. He knew this was the end.

Amy Lewtas (12)
Garstang High School, Garstang

Survival

War was approaching; the army needed everyone who was able to bear weapons to help. The soldiers came and took me away, but not my father, he was too old to fight. I took up weapons and armour. The only battle I will face will be to return alive.

Daniel Knox (12)
Garstang High School, Garstang

Holiday!

I walked down the long, wet runway. As the plane took off I could feel it jolt. It flew from side to side, it seemed like it was in the air for ages but then finally it landed with a bump. I walked out, the sun beamed down on me.

Harry Crooke (12)
Garstang High School, Garstang

The Snatch

I went to call for Harry, he was out. Then I called for James, his dad answered. James and me went to the shop and then we agreed to go to my house. We got to my house, it had been burgled. We opened the door and were kidnapped.

Samuel Anderson (9)
Glenfield Primary School, Glenfield

The Shipwreck

I was on a boat that was taking me home. I was scared I'd fall into the blue sea. I fell asleep later that day. I woke up. I found myself on a beach, an old canoe, a paddle. I paddled all the way home where I met my mum.

Charlie Lomas (8)
Glenfield Primary School, Glenfield

I Am Alone

On the bus, on my own. A creepy old man, about 50, came up to me mysteriously. It was like a ghost town, Bony Borrowtree. The last place I went to I was freaked out by the man. When I got off the bus I heard a dog, a rottweiler.

Tuesday Coleman (8)
Glenfield Primary School, Glenfield

Dark, Dark Boat

There was a dark, dark boat, and in the dark, dark, boat, there was a dark, dark shelf, on the dark, dark shelf, there was a dark, dark cabinet, inside the dark, dark cabinet there was a ghost.

Joshua Scott (8)
Glenfield Primary School, Glenfield

Think

Mum looked at me. I stared back. I didn't know what she was looking at. I froze. At this moment I felt something on my back. When I turned around it was something with a big, black bag. It was him.

Tavia Alonzo (8)
Glenfield Primary School, Glenfield

How Scared Are You?

Abbey was alone, reading in the attic, she heard a *clank!* 'What was that?' she screamed.
Her dad came to sit with her.
Clang!
'Argh!' Dad and Abbey screeched.
Her mum came up.
Bash!
'Argh!' they all screamed.
'Where is Bruv?' said Abbey.
'I don't know!' whispered Mum and Dad.

Matthew Stevens (9)
Glenfield Primary School, Glenfield

Alone

I was sitting down. My mum had gone out. My dad was at work. I was alone. Suddenly I heard something, it sounded like a door. 'Is that you Mum?' I said. 'Is that you Dad?' I said after. There was no sound. I looked, the door was closed.

James Etheridge (9)
Glenfield Primary School, Glenfield

Burgled!

She went to town. *Where shall I go?* she thought, when, *'Stoooooop!'* A man was running with her bag. Another man stepped out. He fell. The police ran to the very frightened lady. The nice man came up to her. 'Here.'

'Thank you,' the lady said.

Bethany Marshall (9)
Glenfield Primary School, Glenfield

Win And Lose

'The big race,' he shouted, 'I'm going to miss it.'
'Calm down it's tomorrow.'
He wouldn't stop. He moaned and shouted, he went mad.
'I'd better get to training right away!' He started to run around the field. I went in. Suddenly, *smash, bang, bang!*

Harry Sharman (9)
Glenfield Primary School, Glenfield

Haunted Wind

The sky went dark and the man walked into the haunted building in the dark country fields, with storms in the sky. He looked through the keyhole, there was an eye. The man slowly opened the door.
'Got ya!'
All that was left was the haunted wind.

Dale Mortimer (11)
Grundisburgh Primary School, Grundisburgh

Eating Plant

John worked at a florist's and looked after a Venus flytrap. He was trying out a new potion but he accidentally dropped it in the Venus flytrap plant. The next morning he walked into where the plant was. As soon as he looked at it ... 'Arrrrgh!'

Callum Lomas (11)
Grundisburgh Primary School, Grundisburgh

The Fiery Screams

I looked at the house through the fog, the fire danced about in front of me. I heard a crash as the front of the house collapsed. I heard wails and screams. But the house had been empty for years!

Becky Holifield (10)
Grundisburgh Primary School, Grundisburgh

Heat Haze

I was hot and sweaty. I looked across the vast sand. There was a heat haze on the horizon. The wind was blowing and the sand started to blow all over me. Later I woke up and wondered how long I had been there. Why hadn't anyone found me?

Emily Witherden (10)
Grundisburgh Primary School, Grundisburgh

Bang

'Come on!' screamed the audience as the cars came racing past.
'And the winner is Ryan Edmunson,' the reporter said with delight.
All of a sudden someone jumped onto the racing track and started dancing. He hadn't realised that the racers were doing a lap for fun. *Bang!*

Jade Cable (11)
Grundisburgh Primary School, Grundisburgh

The Race Of Racers

The best car racers entered a race. They were halfway through the race and about to turn a corner when one racer crashed. The two best drivers were left racing, they were coming up to the finish, they crossed the line and both believed they had won.

George Clark (11)
Grundisburgh Primary School, Grundisburgh

Gravedigger

My heart was beating. I stumbled on some rocks. I fell over and grazed my knee. I turned around and saw my friend running, he was drenched with blood. I opened my eyes in horror and he disappeared.

Ben Buffone (11)
Grundisburgh Primary School, Grundisburgh

Mini Saga

One day I decided to go to the moon, it would test my ability to the max. When I got there, there were weird aliens. I pulled out my gun and shot them, then went home and had burger and chips.

Jamie Strange (11)
Heathcote School, Chingford

To Infinity And Beyond

As they soared past the stars like a cheetah on wheels, they came across a glowing beam. Mr Mcmilliam (a crazy scientist) and his trusty friend Bobblenob (a dog) travelled. As their eyes drew closer they were sucked into the glowing beam. Unfortunately they fell and died!

Kelly Frank (11)
Heathcote School, Chingford

To Infinity And Beyond

One day I went for a walk in the park, when I saw a little green man in a suit. He then took me to his spaceship and put me in this room and he said, 'To infinity and beyond,' and blasted me to outer space. I landed on Earth.

Josh Kimpton (11)
Heathcote School, Chingford

Writing A Mini Saga

One day a man called John Edward was learning about life in space and he set off into space. John went to Mars, he was gathering stardust. John saw something in the mist, it was an alien, he ran to the spaceship and went home. He was delighted.

Tonmie Lee (11)
Heathcote School, Chingford

To Infinity And Beyond

Everyone looked worried except me. 'We'll all pull through fine,' I said, but I knew that wasn't true. Suddenly we were twirling around. Then it was silent. We had been sucked into the black hole like the rest of the world. We would die soon from lack of oxygen. Bye.

Bonnie Jack (12)
Heathcote School, Chingford

Writing A Mini Saga

In space there is an infinity of aliens and strange creatures, with all kinds of things on them. These creatures react strangely to people or animals. One day a person walked in space, then all of a sudden an alien shot a weird object and no one went there again.

Onoufrios Theodoulou (11)
Heathcote School, Chingford

Mini Saga

Johnny English gets into his car and instantly it turned into a rocket, it shot up into the air. He looks out the window and sees Mars. He saw aliens too. He drives into Mars and greets the aliens. He tells them he has to go back to Earth.

Lewis Bannerman
Heathcote School, Chingford

Winning A Mini Saga

One day there were three boys called Brad, Steven and Rob. They were going on a journey up to this cave in the mountain. They started walking up the mountain, when a boulder fell from the mountain, they ran. They carried on walking up and when they got there something happened …

Steven Holmes (11)
Heathcote School, Chingford

Jumps

Suspense before, pressure on my shoulders, people standing behind me waiting impatiently. Thoughts rushing through my brain, have I practised enough, am I really going to do this? Then the final spark of courage runs through me, telling me to do it, then I jump into the icy blue pool.

Niklas Rehmert (13)
International School of Düsseldorf, Germany

The Office

Down dimly lit school corridors, classes with normal, good students all around me. Why can't I be like them? Look at the ground as I walk down the stairs leading to the office. Down, down, down. Door looms in front of me. Daaamn … shouldn't have called him stupid in class!

Nik Baron (13)
International School of Düsseldorf, Germany

Trapped!

Her target flits out of reach, evading her grasp. Spitting in defiance, the quarry glares at his hunter through narrowed eyes. She tries luring him with smooth honeyed tones. 'Come, I won't hurt you.' Swiftly she makes her devious move and seizes him around his scrawny neck. 'Bath time Kitty!'

Malin Bergström (13)
International School of Düsseldorf, Germany

Precious Time

'Ten more minutes, you hear me?'
Heard him? How could I not? What do I do? Only *ten* minutes before my doom! Suddenly, steps on the stairs, coming closer and closer, the door is opening slowly.
'Daaaaad! I'm not tired yet. I want to finish listening to …'
'Now!'

Verena Bethke (13)
International School of Düsseldorf, Germany

Broken Dream

'My favourite room, I can download songs and not pay. I'll sell them; and it makes a lot of money. I'm rich but I'll keep going. Soon the wealthiest man alive; my family should have some cash to live with.'

Knock, knock …
'Who is it?'
'The police …'
'Oh-oh!'

Max Andersen (14)
International School of Düsseldorf, Germany

Pitch-Black

Creeeaaak! Door opens slowly. *Tip-tap,* footsteps, *Whaaat? Tip-tapping* coming closer, faster! Wish Mum would hurry! Curl up, centre of my bed, bury head under covers. Monster's eyes stare at me! 'Snuffles! You dumb dog!'

Carolina Sandbrook (14)
International School of Düsseldorf, Germany

Drowning!

A splash of icy water. My skin contracts from the cold. The air squeezes out of my lungs. I'm drowning! I'm drowning! *Argh!* My mother's voice from far away … 'Get your head out of the sink!'

Martin Shih (13)
International School of Düsseldorf, Germany

The Final Second!

Seconds left on the clock. All I have to do is make one shot and we will be going to the finals! I dash right, then left, pass to Phil and he passes back. I take the shot … swish! The ball goes through. Buzzers and whistles go off … foul!

James Bolton (14)
International School of Düsseldorf, Germany

The Jump

My horse runs faster, faster. I gallop, flying with every step. Soaring, the jump coming closer, closer! My horse goes up, up … I finish, feeling my horse land with a soft step.
'You, you made it!' Everyone's screaming, yelling.
'Whew …' the gold medal dangles from my neck …
'Yay!'

Lisa Jansen (13)
International School of Düsseldorf, Germany

Is It In?

I control the ball, turn to the goal, start sprinting towards it. Their captain slides in. I pull it away, keep going. I decide to have a swing at it. *Boom!* Through the air, right into the back of the net! Goal? *Huh! Why is our goalie in that goal?*

Phil Kelly (14)
International School of Düsseldorf, Germany

Caught Red-Handed

The criminal always returns to the scene of the crime. They won't get away with it this time! I lie in wait, eyes peeled, prepared for a fight! A black figure, this looks suspicious, hand reaching out towards the treasure …
'Lucy, that's the last time you'll raid the cookie jar.'

Clare Leake (13)
International School of Düsseldorf, Germany

Gold Medal

Skates gliding across the glittering ice. Dress flowing to the beat of music. Breath - steady and cold. Across the ring and past the centre. I swing my leg over, pick in the ice, jump, spin twice and land, quickly glancing at the judges, with 10s blurring out of my sight.

Katerina Trefilov (14)
International School of Düsseldorf, Germany

Winning

I can hear the bullets whipping past me. I jump over to the left and twist around to see my opponent. I start firing as I hear another gun go off. I drop them both in a hail of bullets. Everyone moans. I have won another round of *Halo 2*.

Rory Higgins (14)
International School of Düsseldorf, Germany

Trouble

I am waiting for something miserable. It is not the first time. I stand in front of a big wooden door - the principal's office. It *creeeeeps* open.
'It was only a little push.'
'Don't let it happen again!' Mr Martin violently interrupts.
I trot down the corridor, looking for trouble.

Niko Blomeyer (13)
International School of Düsseldorf, Germany

Mini Saga

On the way to the airport Mrs Johnson walked through a wood carrying a small bag. Suddenly a thief stole her bag. The police couldn't do anything and so she missed her plane. 24 hours later she heard that the plane had crashed and all the people were dead . . .

Fiona Schuetze (14)
International School of Paphos, Cyprus

Animal Rescue

After a long, thirsty motorway trip we stopped at a kiosk. I ran towards a noise of a whimpering dog where I found a black, skinny, adorable hunting dog that was stuffed in a dustbin. I gently lifted her out of the bin.

Two months later 'Blackie' joined our family.

Claire Trippit (13)
International School of Paphos, Cyprus

Mini Saga

I met this guy playing football. I asked if I could play. He said, 'Yes.'
I told him I had football boots from a famous player. He asked where I kept them. I told him, then I went home, went to bed.
When I woke up they were gone.

Eliot Gannon (12)
International School of Paphos, Cyprus

Mini Saga

One Sunday afternoon a group of friends were walking when they saw a tall pale man following them. They got scared and began to run.
He was still following and got closer, but when they stopped he passed the girl her phone, which she had dropped beforehand.

Katherine Courtney (14)
International School of Paphos, Cyprus

What Women Go Through!

What was this, the creation on me? It looked more like a torture machine. Hands claw at me, pulling ropes. Choking the air out of me. A foot at my back, another tug. Then it stopped. The torturer smiled, 'My this is graceful. How lovely the corsets made your waist.'

Natalie Kimani (15)
Loreto Convent, Kenya

Tragedy

It had started well with humour and laughter, no doubt we were all going to enjoy it. But somewhere in the middle, tragedy struck. Our hearts sunk, our tears stung our eyes and it suddenly came to an abrupt end.
It was the weirdest movie we had ever watched.

Lydia Gachuhi (16)
Loreto Convent, Kenya

That Very Moment

It was all cosy at first and everything was provided. Something happened and suddenly everyone was screaming for joy and surrounded me. Innocently I cried, now I know better. Gentle hands comforted me gracefully. The undefined start of life, my first encounter with the real world. My birthday!

Sarah Itambo (17)
Loreto Convent, Kenya

Mini Saga

Running was all the tigers seemed to do. They had reached the deep river of Kalp where they roamed free. The hunters stopped when the glowers came up. Orange glowing creatures with knives for pincers and two prickly heads - magically talented. The hunters ran as fast as they could.

Cathryn Antoniadis (12)
Nonsuch High School for Girls, Cheam

The Lady And The Monster

A scream rang out. The howl was issued from an ugly, contorted creature crying on the floor. It shouted a demand to the nearby woman. She weakly objected. It yelled again more fiercely, attracting the attention of strangers. Eventually the mother yielded and bought the chocolate for the spoilt child.

Amy Tiri (13)
Nonsuch High School for Girls, Cheam

As I Woke

I woke up, it was there. Stone-cold face, glaring at mine. The room got colder, the curtains started to wave. I thought it was just the wind; it began to get more forceful, frosty breath.

'No . . .!'

Screams froze in my throat. I didn't believe in ghosts, until then.

Hollie Jones (11)
Our Lady & St Oswald's Catholic Primary School, Oswestry

They Appeared From Nowhere

We wandered down the pathway, into a dark, damp alley. We had been lost for more than an hour. Both of us talked nervously as we started to feel uneasy. We were now walking through a field with overgrown grass. There was a rustle, that was when we were attacked …

Bethany Griffiths (10)
Our Lady & St Oswald's Catholic Primary School, Oswestry

The Kidnap

I was walking home. It was dark and late. I was pushed from behind into a dark alley. I was scared, I didn't know what to do. Heart pounding, I tried to yell but nobody heard me. He grabbed me. I was frozen with fear. Hearing footsteps, he scurried away.

Shannon Graham (10)
Our Lady & St Oswald's Catholic Primary School, Oswestry

The Night I'll Never Forget

My eyes opened.
I heard screams down below, my mum, her face
that of a ghost, pale and ashen.
The windows shattered and the table broke.
She fell. It was gone, the ghost had gone.
Never thought I would be so scared!
Mum's silent, we never spoke of that time again.

Sebastian Pierpoint (10)
Our Lady & St Oswald's Catholic Primary School, Oswestry

A Lucky Escape

Sword breaking, armour broken, lying there helplessly. One phrase in my head, *All hope is lost!* One last boost of strength. Running through the gloomy ruin, skeleton monstrosities. They were quickly disposed of.

Through a door I saw it. The golden eagle.

I quickly grabbed it and was teleported back.

Bradley Wright (10)
Sacred Heart School, Barrow-in-furness

The Haunted Woods

Some people camped out in the haunted woods.
They wanted to see if it was really haunted.
That night they went into the woods but they
were chased out so they ran home.

David Davies (10)
Sacred Heart School, Barrow-in-furness

Backshot

Only three left, Alice, George and Christian. The rest are dead. It'd been a long night running from the troops who shot anything that moved. A soldier appeared. He shot at Alice but George took the bullet and died. Alice cried into the night whilst Christian dropped the smoking gun.

Alice Smith (15)
The Bishop Bell CE Mathematics & Computing Specialist School, Eastbourne

My Adventure Last Tuesday

Down, down, down to the icy caverns! A woodlice crawls across my face and something dark is ahead.
My light flickers.
Suddenly . . . *thump, thumpity thump!*
The something is advancing, closer, louder!
A voice echoes through the caves,
'Get out from under that bed, it's time for tea!'

Laura Upton (15)
The Bishop Bell CE Mathematics & Computing Specialist School, Eastbourne

Death Alley!

We were sprinting. They were catching up. I was getting tired. Someone fell crashing to the ground, whether friend or foe, no time for others. I cut down an alley. I thought they hadn't realised. I was wrong! They approached me.
Smash, I was gone.

Craig Miller (14)
The Bishop Bell CE Mathematics & Computing Specialist School, Eastbourne

Lost

There was nothing but thick, black smoke. Eyes stinging, flesh burning, she crawled searching for an exit. She didn't want to die but as the smoke rapidly filled her lungs, she could see no way out.
'Let her go.' She heard voices full of worry.
Beeeeep! Away into the darkness.

Nikita Butcher (14)
The Bishop Bell CE Mathematics & Computing Specialist School, Eastbourne

Shadows Of The Night

The cloud drifts slowly across the moon, you are plunged into darkness. Scared, alone. The shadows creep inwards blocking you from the outside world. The invisible barrier. The pressure is immense. Suffocating, choking, dying. The moon emerges from the cloud, releasing your pain. Your saviour shining, breaking into your dark.

Tyler North (13)
The Bishop Bell CE Mathematics & Computing Specialist School, Eastbourne

Without A Trace

Normal day. Same lecture. *Boom!* A window blew out. *Boom!* Another went, but after this, silence descended upon the school. Once again *boom!* Glass flew into our faces, everyone was screaming. But the man outside was emotionless. He turned his head, and like the wind, left without a trace.

Joseph Belchem (15)
The Bishop Bell CE Mathematics & Computing Specialist School, Eastbourne

Wild At Heart

I ran and ran. Still running for as far as I could. I turned. No one was there. No one following. Then she was there. In front. Behind. All around me. She moved in closer. Closer. Then she pounced. She squeezed me, opened her mouth and kissed me.

Daniel Bridge (15)
The Bishop Bell CE Mathematics & Computing Specialist School, Eastbourne

Ambush

They stormed the room. Fifty men all armed with guns. Bullets blazing, blood spraying, the soldiers gave no mercy. Room by room they cleared out the terrorists in no time at all.
But then things changed. They were ambushed. Circled in the line of fire. One by one they fell.

Luke Sivers (15)
The Bishop Bell CE Mathematics & Computing Specialist School, Eastbourne

The Quest For Gold

They set out on their voyage to Ethiopia in search of gold - two young lovers, an old sage and their crew. They traversed over the turbulent green seas many a day and many a night. Alas! Only the sage made it to the sought for land on a wooden cask.

Sefeoluwa Oyelude (15)
The International School Ibadan, Nigeria

My Life, Your Life, Our Life, In Life

Ben smiled as he thought of his mother's words, 'This life ends too soon, use it to your satisfaction while it lasts'.
Well yes, I am going to, Ben thought.
Then remembered his father's words,
'Whatever you sow you will reap'.
Ben grimaced then said, 'Life is one huge, difficult maze.'

Akande Rukayat (15)
The International School Ibadan, Nigeria

Can I Make It?

No air. Fear flashed through me like lightning. I kicked but my feet were lead. Blackness closed all around, but my aching body carried on. Just when I should've surely died, my head broke the surface. My lungs filled with copious amounts of cold, salty air. Now I was safe.

Anna de Carteret (13)
The Ladies' College, Guernsey

Protest

There she was, chained to the rusty pole. Who
was going to help her this time?
Suddenly, a hand reached out to her chains.
She screamed as the uniformed stranger
unshackled her and dragged her into his vehicle.
Was this the end? Had her protests been in vain?

Laura Campbell (13)
The Ladies' College, Guernsey

The Sky Is Falling

It was edging closer and closer. Everyone was hypnotised by its power but myself. It was like a crystal fireball hurtling towards the world. Then suddenly a great purple light exploded around us. Then it dawned on me, that this was finally it. The world had come to an end.

Charlotte Bailey (13)
The Ladies' College, Guernsey

Not Bad For Twelve Years Old

Flapping my arms vigorously, I jumped. The cold air smacked me like a rock. I wasn't falling but soaring up to the fluffy clouds. Birds followed me! It was amazing! I flew to the ground. I was now the first ever person to fly. Not bad for twelve years old!

Jocelyn Camm (12)
The Ladies' College, Guernsey

I'm Going To Be Caught

I came to a dead end; I knew I was going to be caught, as the police were chasing me. I would probably be put in prison. I knew I shouldn't have but I wanted the chocolate on Mrs Brown's shelf because it looked so good.

Kelley Cameron (12)
The Ladies' College, Guernsey

We Were All In The War Together

A rat ran past. I didn't have the heart to kill it. We were all in the war together, the Fritz, the rats and us. Suddenly we were ordered over the top. I crawled out the trench, glad to be doing something. That was, until the bullet hit.

Rebecca Ashworth (12)
The Ladies' College, Guernsey

I Was Following Them

There was an unnatural atmosphere in the air; I was following them. They walked briskly around the corner into the unforgiving alley where it hit them: the stench of the rotting corpse.
'Why did you do it?' they asked.
I didn't answer.
They ran and I never saw them again.

Amelia Brown (12)
The Ladies' College, Guernsey

The Blaze

As I walked passed my front door, I spotted red flashing lights. I called Mum. We quickly opened the door. I saw a bright orange blaze! A house was on fire! Everyone gathered outside. Shock blew onto people's faces.
The next day the house was deadly black, silent and bare.

Aimee Gaudion (12)
The Ladies' College, Guernsey

Daddy Didn't Do It

I opened the door. Two policemen stood there.
'Hello little girl. Is Daddy there?'
I stayed silent because the rules to Daddy's game said I couldn't tell them where he was. The man knelt beside me and I told him. Then, Daddy was taken away. I haven't seen him since.

Emma Hardy (13)
The Ladies' College, Guernsey

My Duvet Could Not Save Me Now

I heard the footsteps cease at my door. My heart pumping. The tension was immense.
The handle began to turn; it crept open. In the doorway was the figure. Black as night, eyes, yellow like the sun.
My duvet could not save me now, for I was no longer alone.

Lara Baudains (12)
The Ladies' College, Guernsey

Running

I ran as fast as possible, it following close behind. I knew I couldn't continue much longer. I was condemned to this fate. My legs were slowing, it was catching up. I had to get away. Suddenly, it lunged; something gripped my leg. I was doomed. Then, I woke up.

Katherine Dorrity (12)
The Ladies' College, Guernsey

Oh My God, I'm Going To Die!

Two walls began steadily moving towards me.
I peered desperately; I saw the walls had metal
spikes. 'Oh my God, I'm going to die!' I screamed.
I continued screeching until there was a blinding
light, a curtain went up and a man said,
'Don't worry, it was only a joke!'

Katie Enevoldsen (12)
The Ladies' College, Guernsey

Below The Water

I couldn't surface the water. I was kicking frantically and yet just sinking further down. My breath was getting short, my vision was blurred. I tried to scream but the water swallowed my voice. I hit the tiled floor and lay helplessly.
If I wasn't rescued, soon I would die.

Chloe Davison (13)
The Ladies' College, Guernsey

The Scream Echoed

A blood-curdling scream echoed from the kitchen. She lay motionless on the cold tiled floor. The creature glared at me with its glistening red eyes. Its face was as white as freshly fallen snow. Its lips were deep red, dripping with blood.
It was then that it turned on me.

Melanie Ayres (12)
The Ladies' College, Guernsey

The Damp, Dark Dungeon Of Lions

Down into the damp, dark dungeon she tumbled. Nobody would hear Mia's mournful cries again. The lions roared with delight, showing their jagged canines soon to be stained with blood. They pierced Mia's silky skin as her golden locks were ripped from her skull. The lions had devoured their lunch.

Sarah Le Mesurier (12)
The Ladies' College, Guernsey

Ghost Ship

A battleship, floating above dark grey Atlantic waters, waves crashing against the bow. Silence. The men, now quivering wrecks, flew below decks clutching pictures of their sweethearts, saying silent prayers. The German ghost ship was looming. Men fell silent as the spirit passed through them. They never had a chance.

Niamh Hanna (12)
The Ladies' College, Guernsey

Diamonds

We were walking along the narrow lane, the wind blowing in our faces. It was very peaceful until we stumbled over a bag. Inside was shiny, solid diamonds. We picked up the bag and fled to the police. The bag was filled with over a million pounds worth of diamonds.

Charlotte Giles (13)
The Ladies' College, Guernsey

Not Home!

When I got home, Sally wasn't there. I made my tea and watched my programme. Sally still wasn't home and I started to get worried. I looked down the road. No sign of her. I got ready for bed. Then I heard the door open, it was Sally my cat.

Amy Baird (11)
The Ladies' College, Guernsey

The KitKat Wrapper

He glanced down to see a gorgeous shiny substance flapping in the wind. The object started blowing away, catching the beaming sun as it went. He followed the substance for hours on end, finally managing to catch it. Magpies from all around still come to see the beautiful shining prize.

Rebecca Case (11)
The Ladies' College, Guernsey

A New Friend

I had been longing to know what it was *all* day at school. I rushed home, thinking about nothing but my surprise. I opened the front door and was nearly knocked over whilst being covered in loads of friendly licks. A beautiful little dog all of my own!

Laura Bampton (10)
The Ladies' College, Guernsey

The Race Is On

Ape man was first trying to climb over the hill; he saw ape girl behind him. He rushed up and fell down again! Ape girl had now taken the lead. Ape man was not pleased. He ran as fast as he could, tripped over a stone and lost.

Fenella Gladstone (11)
The Ladies' College, Guernsey

War

We were going to war. We lined up, all smart and proud. Off we went. Suddenly, it was not so great. people I knew were dying. But I couldn't concentrate on that. My horse reared as I plunged my sword through a man. Their king.
I had killed their king.

Kirsten Anderson (12)
The Ladies' College, Guernsey

My Daughter

I was walking along one day, when I heard a cry; the sound led to a bush. I reached out and felt a child. I attempted lifting her out. She would not move, she was trapped! I called 999 and they got her out. She is now my adopted daughter.

Sophie Caseby (11)
The Ladies' College, Guernsey

Mini Saga

I have just arrived at the battlefield. I feel sick and my hands shake with fear. What will become of me? Will I survive?
The battle begins and I fight bravely. I'm exhausted but alive.
I'm on the way home, when I hear plans for the next battle . . .

Josh Richards (10)
Threemilestone School, Truro

The Barbecue

I saw it. A monster. It gazed at me. I picked up a stone with my hand and I thrust it in the air. *Clang!* A sour noise. It's going to eat me. I ran away, but as the light turned on I saw it was just . . . the . . . barbecue.

Jordan Hansen (10)
Threemilestone School, Truro

The Dog

There it was, standing in front of me; I moved back two paces, the dog moved two paces forward. The weirdest thing was that there was a line joining us together. All of a sudden I realised it was just my shadow.

Craig Jackson (10)
Threemilestone School, Truro

The Nappy

As I crept into the bedroom I looked in and saw a bright light. Carefully I tiptoed to the bed and on the other side there was a nappy. But I had no brothers or sister!
I opened the en suite door and there was Toby, next-door's son.

James Benney (11)
Threemilestone School, Truro

Mini Saga

She stood, waiting for their opinion, scared of what they might think. She quivered. Her heart pounding, her breathing raspy. She screamed but no sound came. The audience clapped, 'Encore!'

Bethany Howell (10)
Threemilestone School, Truro

Mini Saga

I am panting and puffing, am I going to make it? My legs feel like they are going to give way. I have one more step to go; on the running machine!

Lisa Caddy (10)
Threemilestone School, Truro

The Classroom

I walked into the classroom dreading what I might find. Then I see it, the thing I feared. Then it started. I couldn't escape from it. I couldn't think of anything. I didn't know what to do. I didn't know how to spell a word for my spelling test.

William Bowden (10)
Threemilestone School, Truro

The Figure

The bedroom was dark. I peered round. A lumpy figure stood by my bed. 'Come out!' No answer. My heart pounded. I picked up a toy. I threw it. It didn't move. I took a step back. Fumbled for the light. Blinked, sighed. It was my dressing gown!

Sabina Moss (11)
Threemilestone School, Truro

Do I Have To?

I could hear the high-pitched squeak of a furry blood-sucking creature, the smell alone was bad enough. I got closer, closer, the creature's teeth grinding on a carrot. Its teeth showing and its house wet and soggy.
'Mum do I have to clean out the guinea pigs?'

Jack Dyer (10)
Threemilestone School, Truro

Mini Saga!

I leaned against the metal ladder of my bunk, my head tilted right back. Claws were piercing into my neck. I tried to push it away. I knew that I had no chance to escape.
'No, please Kitty! I know you're happy but no need to dribble all over me!'

Jessica Hyland (10)
Threemilestone School, Truro

The Champion

I had done it, I had beaten the master at his own game. I would be king of the world. Now I had beaten him; I only had to beat one, two, three, four … one thousand two hundred and thirty-five people. Oh, who am I kidding, I hate chess!

Nikita Vasistha
Waldegrave School for Girls, Twickenham

True Or False?

There it was. I'd seen it again. If I didn't get the critical footage of that unnatural being, then I was dead meat. But this time I wasn't going to miss it, and I didn't. I'd captured the perfect picture and proved that the Loch Ness monster was real!

Georgia Hirst (13)
Waldegrave School for Girls, Twickenham

Information

We hope you have enjoyed reading this book - and that you will continue to enjoy it in the coming years.
If you like reading and writing, drop us a line or give us a call and we'll send you a free information pack. Alternatively visit our website at www.youngwriters.co.uk

Write to:
Young Writers Information,
Remus House,
Coltsfoot Drive,
Peterborough,
PE2 9JX
Tel: (01733) 890066
Email: youngwriters@forwardpress.co.uk